ANIMALS IN THE ALPHABET

PAINTINGS BY CARLA'S FUNKY ART

Dedicated to Dana Erb,
for giving me the idea to make this book,
Mahalo! Special thanks to Daniel Seaton,
for always believing in me and my art, and your
countless hours of work on this book. Last but
not least, to Tony "The Fly Whisperer" Locke for
putting the whole thing together.

A is for these two

Amazingly

Awesome

Affectionate

Alpacas

B

is for this little

Bold

Brown

Busy

Beaver

C is for a couple of

Charmingly

Clumsy

Camels

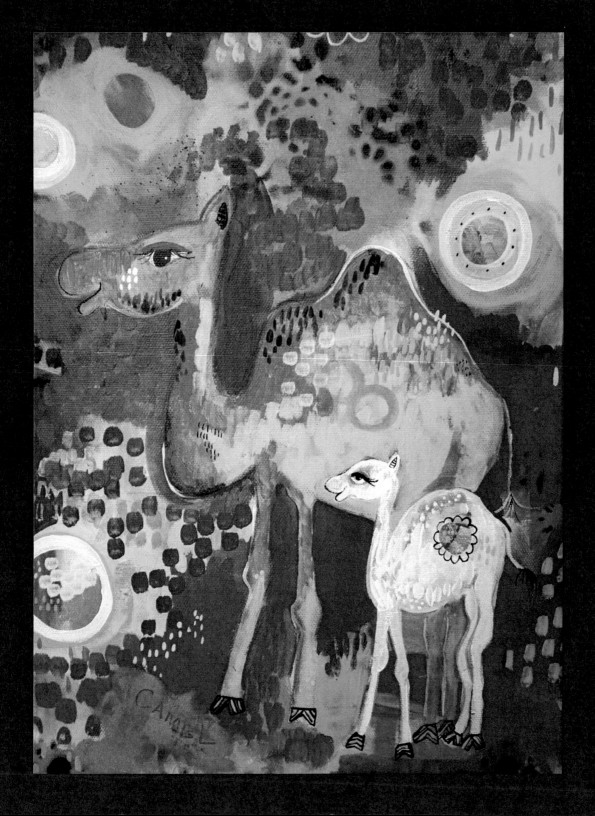

D is for these two

Darling

Dreamy

Dazzling

Ducks

E is for an

Endearing

Excited

Energetic

Elephant

F is for this

Furry

Feisty but

Friendly

Fox

G is for a

Gloriously

Grand

Graceful

Giraffe

H is for a couple of

Handsome

Happy

Hedgehogs

I is for one

Intelligently

Interesting

Iguana

J is for this

Jetting

Jeweled

Jazzy

Jellyfish

K is for a

Kind

Khaki

Kangaroo

L is for these

Longish

Looking

Loveable

Llamas

M is for a

Magnificently

Marvelous

Masculine

Moose

ZEBRA TAKES THE TRAIN

Words by Mr. Krieb   Pictures by Linda Smythe

Puddle Jump Books

ISBN 978-0-9961795-1-5

SEAT

♦ Z ♦

All aboard!

Zebra just bought his ticket.
Now, it's time for him to board the train.
This will be his very first train ride!
Let's see if he can find his seat!

Zebra's going to take the train.
His suitcase is all packed.

He's off to visit grandmama,
who lives in Hackensack.

He taxis to the station, his handbag in his hoof. The station is quite beautiful. It has a Spanish roof.

He checks the daily schedule.
His train will leave at nine. He'd better get his
ticket. He'd better get in line.

Now it's time to board the train.
It's time to move tout de suite.

He climbs into car No. 1
and tries to find his seat.

Squeezing by some big Ape, who's halfway in the aisle.
Excuse me, Mrs. Bear, but could you get your child?
He's down here on the floor with baby Crocodile.

Dog is sleeping like a log already,
goodness me!
Even old man Elephant is comfy as can be.

Good grief! The train is moving,
and I'm still on my feet! Where's my seat?

Flamingo has a sandwich. She gives Giraffe a bite.
Mr. Hippo's playing checkers with Iguana on the right.

Jellyfish and Kangaroo are talking politics.
Leopard's showing Mackerel a few of his card tricks.

Conductor says,"We'll make a stop in Memphis, Tennessee. Please don't leave your seat," he says. Hey! What about me?

I think I see an empty seat! . . .
Oh, I'm sorry, Madam Newt.
How could I not have noticed you in your designer suit?

Now my legs are slow, my head hangs low, my eyes are on
the blink. Excuse me, Mrs. Octopus, but could I have
a drink? . . . Porcupine does needlepoint.

It's starting to get warm. Quail is frail,
and Rat, his nurse, is in her uniform.
"We must be in Jersey," I hear Skunk telling Toad.

My suitcase now is dragging like a two-ton overload!
Umbrella bird looks up at me -
her pity plainly shows.

Vulture, very cultured, plays opera in his ears.
Weasel watches out the window as,
at last, my seat appears!

I'm just about to settle in, when Xenops says
to Yak, "Well, here we are, my friend.
We're in Hackensack!"

With a love for art, I illustrated workbooks, painted posters, and taught children's art programs before teaching third grade for twenty years. In my classroom, I always encouraged young artists! Now retired from teaching, I still love to draw and paint and use recycled materials for creative expression.

Linda Smythe

For thirty fantabulous years, I created lessons for, and taught, Gifted and Talented Education (GATE) students in California. For twenty of those magical years, I also taught kindergarten. All the while, I was writing stories and songs for children. Stories and songs that are perfect for Puddle Jump Books!

Mr. Krieb

Made in the USA
San Bernardino, CA
17 November 2015

N is for a couple of

Nice

Nutty

Narwhals

O is for these

Odd

Ominous

Ostriches

P is for a

Powerful

Passing

Polar bear

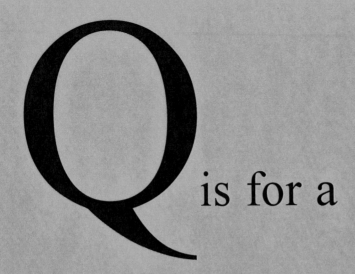

Q is for a

Quick

Quaint

Quail

R is for these

Ridiculously

Risky

Rascal

Racoons

S is for a family of

Soft

Swift

Serene

Swans

T is for this

Thrilling

Tough

Tiger

V is for a

Vivid

Vocal

Vulture

W is for these two

Wonderfully

Wacky

Walruses

X is for a school of

Xenial

X-ray tetra fish

Y is for a

Youthful

Yak

Z is for two

Zany

Zealous

Zebras

Color Me

Made in the USA
San Bernardino, CA
17 November 2015